Daniel Feels One Stripe Nervous

Includes Strategies to Cope with Feeling Worried

Adapted by Alexandra Cassel Schwartz
Based on the screenplay "Daniel's Substitute Teacher"
Written by Jill Cozza-Turner and Alexandra Cassel Schwartz
Poses and layouts by Jason Fruchter

SIMON SPOTLIGHT

An imprint of Simon and Schuster Children's Publishing Division • New York London Toronto Sydney New Delhi
1230 Avenue of the Americas, New York, New York 10020 • This Simon Spotlight paperback edition December 2020
© 2020 The Fred Rogers Company • All rights reserved, including the right of reproduction in whole or in part in any form.
SIMON SPOTLIGHT and colophon are registered trademarks of Simon & Schuster, Inc. • For information about special discounts for
bulk purchases, please contact Simon & Schuster Special Sales at 1-866-506-1949 or business@simonandschuster.com
Manufactured in the United States of America 1020 LAK • 10 9 8 7 6 5 4 3 2 1
ISBN 978-1-5344-8799-4 • ISBN 978-1-5344-8800-7 (eBook)

It was a beautiful day in the neighborhood. Daniel was so excited to sing with his class in a show for all the grown-ups!

"I can't wait to get to school because Teacher Harriet is going to teach us a dance to go along with our song!" Daniel said.

"Well, then let's dance our way to Trolley!" Mom Tiger said.

"Teacher Harriet! Teacher Harriet!" Daniel called out as he ran to the school door. "I'm ready for the show!"

But when Daniel walked into the room, he was surprised to see that Teacher Harriet wasn't there!

"Hello! I'm Mr. Malik," said the substitute teacher. "You must be Daniel Tiger."

Daniel was confused. He had never seen Mr. Malik before! Daniel moved closer to his mom.

Mom sang,

♪ ♫ *"Ask questions about what's happening. It might help."* ♪ ♫

"My question is . . . ," Daniel began, "where's Teacher Harriet?" Daniel was worried about her.

"Teacher Harriet wasn't feeling well, so she stayed home to rest. But she should be back tomorrow," Mr. Malik explained.

But Daniel still felt worried. "What about our song?" he asked. "Can we still sing?"

"You sure can," said Mr. Malik. "Teacher Harriet told me all about the show, so I've been getting everything ready!"

That made Daniel feel a little better.

Mom kneeled down next to Daniel. "Even though school might feel different, you can still have a great day!" she said.
They sang,

♪ ♫ *"Things may change, and that's okay.* ♪ ♫
Today we can do things a different way!"

It was time for Mom to leave, but she would be back later to see Daniel's show. She gave Daniel a big hug and sang,

♪ ♪ *"Grown-ups come back."* ♪ ♪

It was time for Daniel and his friends to practice for the show. Mr. Malik was excited to hear their song!

"Teacher Harriet always plays her guitar to tell us when it's time to start singing," Prince Wednesday explained.

"I don't play the guitar," Mr. Malik said.

Daniel felt worried again. How would they sing their song without the guitar?

Mr. Malik began to sing. Then he grabbed a harmonica.

*♪ ♪ "Things may change, and that's okay.
Today we can do things a different way!" ♪ ♪*

He may not play the guitar like Teacher Harriet, but he *does* play an instrument!

As Mr. Malik played his harmonica, the children began to sing.

♪ ♪ *"Bright, bright sunshine, growing flowers,* ♪ ♪
birdies, too! Birdies, too! . . ."

The song sounded great. "But we still don't have a dance," Daniel said. "Teacher Harriet was supposed to teach us a dance today!"

"Hmm . . . I may not be Teacher Harriet," Mr. Malik began, "but I'm sure we can come up with something." Mr. Malik helped the kids rehearse some dance moves.

Katerina wiggled her fingers,

O the Owl flapped his wings,

Miss Elaina jumped backward,

Jodi and Prince Wednesday shook their shoulders,

and Daniel gave himself a great big hug!

Soon the grown-ups arrived and took their seats.
"Is everyone ready?" Mr. Malik asked the class.
"Not Jodi," O the Owl said.

Jodi was feeling a little nervous. She was worried about singing and dancing in front of so many neighbors!

"Teacher Harriet always helps me feel better, but she isn't here today," Jodi said.

"Sometimes I feel a little nervous, too," Mr. Malik told her. He gave Jodi a special, invisible, brave coat. "If you put it on and zip it up, you might feel a little braver."

Jodi tried it, and sure enough, she *did* feel a little bit braver!

Soon it was time for the show! Mr. Malik played his harmonica, and the kids began to sing and dance:

♪ ♪ *"Bright, bright sunshine, growing flowers,* ♪ ♪
birdies, too! Birdies, too! . . ."

The grown-ups clapped and cheered, and the students took their bows. Mr. Malik was so proud of Daniel's class.

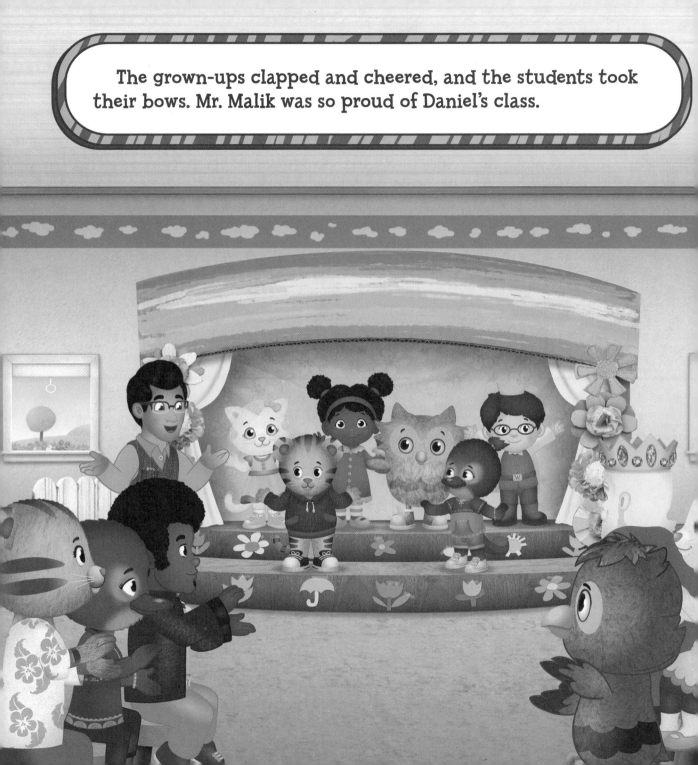

If you're ever feeling nervous
or worried, you can sing these songs.
Singing might make you feel better, too!

When we do something new,
let's talk about what we'll do.

Give a squeeze, nice and slow.
Take a deep breath, and let it go.

When you're upset,
you can find a way to feel better.

Close your eyes,
and think of something happy.

It helps to say what you're feeling.

When something is new,
holding a hand can help you.

It's okay to feel sad
sometimes. Little by little,
you'll feel better again.

"We all missed Teacher Harriet," Daniel began, "but doing things a different way turned out to be okay! Ugga Mugga."